Benji

BENJI ON THE ROAD

Published by Scholastic Inc., *Publishers since 1920.* SCHOLASTIC and associated logos are trademarks and/or registered trademarks of Scholastic Inc.

ISBN 978-1-338-21222-8

10 9 8 7 6 5 4 20 21 22

Printed in the U.S.A. 40
First printing, 2018

Benji

BENJI ON THE ROAD

by Mary Tillworth

Scholastic Inc.

CHAPTER 1

It was a hot night in a sleepy Louisiana town, and a bright-eyed puppy named Benji was getting ready to pounce. He crouched in a brick alley behind a pizza parlor, nose quivering. An old green dumpster rained paint chips and rust flakes over his golden fur. A stack of flattened cardboard boxes tied up with twine lay nearby.

Benji had played with his brothers in the alley all day, but now his attention was on more serious matters. He was on the hunt for dinner. His black-tipped ears stood up and he cocked his head to one side as he listened for long, shuffling steps.

After a few minutes, the human Benji had been waiting for appeared. He was a gangly teenager, with cropped brown hair spiked with gel and short, scraggly hairs growing out of his chin. He sported a backward baseball cap and a pair of earphones, and he was dragging a thick black garbage bag behind him.

When the kid reached the dumpster, he dropped the trash bag and lifted up the dumpster lid. Bending down, he grasped the top of the bag with both hands and heaved it into the dumpster.

Before the kid could drop the dumpster lid, Benji made his move. He leapt out from his hiding place, barking in soft, short yips. He shook his head, his floppy ears thumping to and fro. His long brown tail flicked back and forth.

"Hey, there!" the pizza boy exclaimed. He removed his earphones and reached down to pet Benji. Just as his hand was about to brush the top of Benji's head, Benji ducked and scurried back. He barked playfully.

"Come back here!" the kid said, laughing.

Benji drew back, his tail wagging madly. As the kid stepped toward him, he bolted. Ignoring his mother's warning growl to come back, Benji ran out to the sidewalk. As the pizza boy gave chase, Benji led him around the corner and down the main street. He scampered past shops closing down for the night, and dodged giant metal animals that honked and screeched as they swerved away from him.

They went several streets before the kid stopped. "Hey, I gotta get back to work," he told Benji, panting.

Benji trotted up and let the kid scratch behind his ears. When he was done, the kid stood up reluctantly and headed back to the pizza parlor. After waiting a few minutes, Benji did the same.

When he reached the alley, his tail wagged happily. Everything had gone exactly as planned. After being closed for days, the heavy lid to the dumpster was finally open. In his eagerness to chase Benji, the pizza boy had forgotten to close it.

Benji scrambled up the pile of cardboard boxes. At the top, he teetered for a moment before jumping headfirst into the open dumpster.

Using his tiny claws, he tore into the garbage bags. When he was finally able to make holes big enough to dig the food out, it was as if he had landed in stray-puppy heaven. In the first bag, he found half-eaten pizza crusts and tomato sauce. Another bag was full of stale donuts covered with cinnamon and sugar, or glazed with icing. Still a third held apple cores, banana peels, bruised peaches, and overripe strawberries. It was more than enough food to feed a scrawny puppy—and his hungry family, too.

Benji lifted his head and barked. From the end of the alley, his mother trotted out from the makeshift shelter she had created from discarded trash. Benji's brothers and sisters tumbled out behind her. As Benji tossed food over the lip of the dumpster, he could hear his mom and his siblings crunching down on the feast.

When he was sure his family had had enough to eat, Benji licked his lips and burrowed his nose into the nearest trash bag. He gobbled up the first thing he saw—a juicy strawberry with fuzzy green mold on the top. It tasted delicious. He chomped into a donut and then wolfed down three pizza crusts. When he was done, he settled down on a soft trash bag and closed his eyes. He fell asleep to the happy gurgling of his tummy.

He woke to the pattering of rain thrumming down on the metal around him. In the dim light that spilled out from the streetlamps, Benji could see big, wet drops bouncing onto the trash bags and running down, leaving dark streaks on the black plastic.

Somewhere nearby, a door slammed. Benji shook the sleep and rain from his eyes and stood up. Something was wrong. Usually he could hear the gentle woof of his mom and the yelping of his brothers and sisters as they bickered and fought. But alone in the dumpster, he could hear nothing.

Suddenly, he heard a growl. It was his mother. Normally she growled gently if her pups strayed too far from her sight, but this growl was different. He had never heard it before. It was deep and menacing, but also held an edge of fear.

Benji scrambled up the piles of trash bags and lifted his head out of the dumpster. He could see two men coming down the alley. One of them was holding a long pole with a loop at the end. As he approached the dumpster, Benji ducked out of sight, but not before he saw the man swing the pole toward the ground.

There was a sharp bark, followed by a yelp.

"Gotcha!" crowed the man.

Benji lifted his head up again and saw the man leading his mom forward. The loop had tightened around her neck. She dug her claws into the hard pavement, trying desperately to pull back, but she was no match for the much heavier human. As he tugged her forward, the man's partner reached down and gathered Benji's brothers and sisters into a kennel. He slammed the metal door shut and then lifted the kennel into the back of a van, where the other man had already put Benji's mom. Once the dogs were stowed away, the man with the pole threw it next to the kennels and shut the back doors. He inserted a key and locked them.

Chuckling, the two men got into the front of the van. As they started the engine, Benji hurtled off the dumpster. As he scrambled down the cardboard pile, the van peeled away in a cloud of smoke and burnt rubber.

Benji hopped to the ground and took off after

the van. Barking wildly, he followed it down the streets, keeping it in sight until it turned a corner onto a main road that led out of town. As it hit a straightaway, the van shifted gears. It gained speed and rumbled away into the night.

Benji stopped running. As the rain fell softly around him, he stood perfectly still. He was alone for the first time in his life, and he didn't know what to do.

Ahead of him was a long, dark road where his family had disappeared into the distance. Behind him were the comforting lights of the town he knew, and an open dumpster that had enough food to keep him fed for weeks.

Benji's mouth watered as he remembered the ripped-open trash bags and the heaps and heaps of treats inside them. But then he thought about his mom and his siblings, scared and howling in the van, and his heart began to thump. He couldn't leave them to their fate. He had to try to save them.

Benji took a small, slow breath. Then he trotted into the darkness and onto the unknown road ahead of him.

CHAPTER 2

Benji followed the road for hours. Finally, when the rain turned into a downpour that soaked him to the bone, he found shelter underneath a small stone bridge. Curled up in a wet, shivering ball, he tried his best to fall asleep.

For the next week, Benji kept on the road. Gradually, the small towns and fields he went through gave way to neighborhoods with far more houses and far fewer flowers. And then, one morning, the neighborhoods turned into an ocean of buildings that reached endlessly into the sky, connected by hot concrete sidewalks with not a patch of grass in sight.

Benji had only known the small, cozy place where he had been born. Now every alley was strange. The first one he poked his nose into was full of hissing rats that looked like they could have bitten off his nose if he had gotten too close. The second held a yowling gang of street cats who did not seem interested in sharing their space with a stray puppy.

It wasn't much better out in the open. The streets had far more of the roaring metal animals on them, speeding by and honking loudly as if they were constantly angry. And there were a lot more humans, too. They seemed to be in much more of a hurry than the humans Benji had known in his little hometown. These city humans clicked and clacked across the streets in a noisy rush.

Worse than the noise was that Benji always felt like there were eyes watching him. Back home, he had been able to dig in garbage cans for food without anyone looking. Now, if he even sniffed at one of the large metal city wastebaskets, a shouting human would send him hurrying away. Benji realized that in order to eat, he would have to find food in places other than the trash.

It was early afternoon when he hit the jackpot. He came across a large brick building with several double doors where hundreds of school kids were flooding out onto a large, fenced-in playground. As they played games and chatted with one another, they pulled out snacks from their pockets and began munching on them.

Benji's eyes lit up. He spotted a tall chain-link

door in the fence. Although it was closed, he was able to squeeze through the space between the door and the fence. Trotting around, Benji began begging cookies and crackers from the students.

He was enjoying a sticky caramel that a student had tossed to him when he saw a skinny, freckled kid with green eyes and a mop of brown curls on his head. The kid was holding a bag of popcorn in one hand and a well-worn guitar in the other. He was talking to a girl with short hair and two shiny gold hoops in each of her ears. All of a sudden, the boy thrust the guitar out to the girl. She shook her head and pushed it back toward him.

Benji saw a piece of popcorn drop to the ground. He chewed and swallowed the last bit of caramel and trotted toward the two students. He was about to nudge the boy's hand in hopes of making more popcorn fall, when the girl suddenly grabbed the boy, pulling him toward her. "You gotta stand up for yourself, Harry!" she said.

Harry drew back, clutching the guitar to his chest. "I can't, Riley," he said. "I'm not as big as Sam and his gang, or as strong. And it's not worth making them mad."

"Music is *everything* to you. I've heard you play when you're not being bullied. You're good, and it's worth it," Riley replied.

Harry just shook his head. "You don't understand

what it's like to be scared all the time. If I never play again and they leave me alone, I'm okay with that." He held the guitar out again. "Please. Just take my guitar and keep it safe. I don't want anything to happen to it."

Riley folded her arms. "One day you're going to realize that you're tougher than them."

"Well, that day isn't today," said Harry.

Riley sighed. "Fine. I'll keep your guitar safe." She reached out and took the guitar. "But really, Harry. You deserve better than what you give yourself." She turned and walked away.

Harry sighed. He slumped down onto the ground.

Benji trotted up to him. Whining softly, he gently nuzzled Harry's hand.

"Oh, hey, pup!" Harry looked at Benji in surprise. He patted Benji's head awkwardly. "You hungry?"

Benji woofed.

Harry tipped out a handful of popcorn and scattered it on the ground. Almost before the last piece had dropped from his fingertips, Benji had gobbled everything up. He licked his lips happily.

"You're *really* hungry, aren't you?" Harry looked carefully at Benji. "Poor pup. You look like you haven't eaten for days." He turned the bag upside down, shaking all the popcorn out.

Benji dove into the pile. In a flash, it was gone.

He had a piece of popcorn stuck in his teeth, but he didn't care. He jumped on Harry and cleaned the kid's face in thanks.

Harry laughed and put his hands out to stop Benji, but it was no use. He got a full-on doggie face bath before he was able to pluck the puppy up and hold him away from him. "You're welcome," he told Benji.

"Hey, loser!" a voice called from across the playground.

Harry dropped Benji and stood up. Benji could see his knees shaking through his jeans. "What do you want, Sam?" he said. His voice sounded thin and scared.

A boy with meaty fists and thick blond hair had come up to Harry. Behind him were three boys with smaller fists and scowls on their faces.

"I want to talk to you about today's music class," said Sam. "You know, the part where you tried to show off on your guitar? That was not cool, man." He jabbed a thumb into Harry's chest. "You think you're all that, don't you? Some kind of musical genius? I bet you can't even play expert on *Guitar Hero*."

"He's more like a guitar *weirdo*," chimed in one of the kids behind Sam.

"Good one, Leo," sniggered Sam.

"Hey, I didn't mean anything by it," Harry said. His voice was trembling. "I just like music, that's all. And when the music teacher asked me to perform—"

"Don't interrupt me!" roared Sam. "What I'm trying to tell you is that playing music is stupid. And for your own good, you should never play again." His voice got soft. "And when I say never, I mean *never*. If you don't agree, well, then, we're gonna have to teach you a lesson. And it won't be musical."

"Get him, Sam!" crowed another kid.

Before Sam could reply, Harry took off. He raced to the edge of the playground and began climbing the metal fence that surrounded it. Sam jumped up and grabbed Harry's shoe. Harry pulled himself up, and the shoe came flying off. He vaulted over the top of the fence and hopped onto the sidewalk.

As Sam and the other three boys climbed the fence, Benji raced to the other end of the playground. He ran out the door and then bolted in the direction of where Harry had gone. He reached Harry just as the other boys jumped down onto the sidewalk.

Harry zigzagged through the streets, half hopping with his one shoe, desperately trying to shake the bullies. Benji ran behind him, peeking back to see how close their pursuers were. Harry ducked into an alleyway and crouched behind a line of garbage cans.

Thinking quickly, Benji launched himself onto one of the cans, making it tilt forward and spill dirty plastic bags onto the ground. He ripped open the bags. Waves of stinky garbage smell filled the air.

Benji dove under the garbage and hid just as the bullies rushed by. They stopped in front of the alley.

"He might have gone down there," said one of the kids.

Sam plugged his nose. "Ugh! No one would hide in that alley with that stench. C'mon, guys. I bet he's around the next corner."

As the boys raced away, Benji emerged from the smelly heap of trash. He trotted to the back of the alley and rejoined Harry.

"Hey, thanks, pooch," said Harry. He poked his head out of the alley to make sure the coast was clear and then led Benji in the opposite direction the boys had gone, to a three-story apartment building at the end of a quiet, tree-lined street.

"Thanks for helping me out, little guy," he told Benji. "I'd love to let you in for the night, but you gotta stay outside. Ever since I can remember, my dad has been scared of germs, and he won't let any animals inside. No cats or dogs—not even a Chihuahua." He patted Benji's head and then jogged up the stoop stairs leading to his home. He gave Benji a final wave, then went inside and firmly shut the door.

As he heard the lock click in place, a wave of loneliness washed over Benji. He knew there was probably a good reason why he hadn't been let inside, but it still felt like he was being abandoned all over again. He whined sadly, looking to see if the door would open.

When it didn't, he turned away sadly and headed back into the night.

CHAPTER 3

After dark, the city was a whole different world. Many of the streets were lit by tall lamps that dotted the sidewalks. Lights blazed out of office buildings and tall apartment complexes. But despite all the brightness, the alleys were dark.

Benji passed orange-and-white pipes that blew hot white smoke into the night. Broken glass glittered on the ground where he stepped, and several times he had to swerve out of the way of humans who wove in jagged, uneven lines down the street. He was nervous and scared—every bright light felt like it was showing something best kept in the shadows.

As the long hours passed, Benji's tail began to droop. Just when he thought he couldn't walk any farther, he came to an alley that was empty except for a few metal garbage cans. Benji gave a short bark to see if any creature was around.

No one barked or meowed or hissed or shouted back. He pawed at the ground, then turned three times before flopping down behind the garbage can farthest from the street. His nose dropped onto his paws and he closed his eyes. He was content. At last, he had found a safe place to settle down for the night.

A moment later, he was awoken by the sound of metal sliding across metal. He looked up, rolled away, and then scrambled to his feet just as the can lid came crashing down right over the spot where he had been sleeping. Benji backed away a few steps. His legs tensed, and he was ready to bolt out of the alley if a gigantic, enraged stray dog came out of the can.

A nose poked out, and a yipping ball of fur launched itself at Benji. Benji yelped and drew back. He stood looking down at the tiny Chihuahua who was barking frantically at him, trying to nip his toenails off.

Benji bent down. Gently, he touched his nose to the Chihuahua's. Surprised, the tiny dog stopped barking. Benji gently laid back down on the ground and rolled onto his side. The little dog paused. Then she trotted over and snuggled down next to him. Smiling, Benji went to sleep.

* * *

The next morning, Benji awoke to a growling tummy. He stretched, and his foot bumped into a tiny ball of fur. The Chihuahua blinked open her eyes and smiled at Benji. Her stubby little tail thumped happily.

Benji got to his feet and took a good look at the alley. In the morning light, it was simple and cozy, with tidy walls and plenty of space to stretch out. Benji thought it would do just fine for a place to stay.

It was time to find breakfast. He trotted to the end of the alley and looked out. Across the busy street he saw a bakery. Through its tall glass windows, he saw loaves of bread piled high and platters of sweets that made his mouth water.

Benji looked back at the Chihuahua. He pointed to the alley entrance with his nose.

The Chihuahua timidly followed Benji toward the street. But when two humans walked by, she gave a yelp of fear and skittered back to the safety of her garbage can. Benji tried to give her a little nudge, but she wouldn't move. He would have to find breakfast himself.

He checked to make sure there weren't any cars coming before running across the road. The bakery door was shut, but soon a customer came out holding a long, crispy loaf of bread.

Benji flew toward the bakery. As the customer

swung the door shut, he sprang forward and darted inside.

He saw a row of tables next to a large display case and ducked under an empty one. He knew he had to act fast before someone spotted him and shooed him out. Underneath another table, he spotted a hunk of bread that had been dropped. He snatched it with his teeth and then squeezed out when another customer entered the store.

He rejoined the little dog in the alley and tore the bread in two with his paws. Together the two dogs ate their breakfast in the early morning light.

Benji's second target was a food truck selling burgers and fries two blocks down from the alley. He found a perfect hiding spot behind a rear wheel of the truck and waited.

For a while, all he saw were shoes. Then he heard a small shout of surprise from the counter. A handful of fries dropped to the ground.

Benji scurried out from behind the big black tire and swooped over the fries. A moment later, they disappeared. He licked his lips and retreated under the truck. He was able to get another two handfuls of fries and a piece of burger before a big, sweaty head bent down to face him behind the tire. The head started to yell, and Benji decided it was time for a new hunting ground.

Toward evening, he returned to the alley. The tiny dog greeted him with yips and licks. Benji smiled and dropped a piece of burger he had been saving for his friend. That night they went to bed with tummies that rumbled, but only a little.

CHAPTER 4

The next day Benji woke up before the little Chihuahua. Carefully sliding back so as not to wake his friend, he pulled himself to his feet and headed out in the early morning light.

The bakery wasn't open yet, and the food truck had not yet pulled up to the curb. Benji decided to go farther out from his alley to look for breakfast. He trotted down several streets but didn't find anything promising.

As he rounded a corner, he came across the first patch of green he had seen in the city. There was a gentle hill covered in benches and trees, with a swept path that threaded through it.

Benji sniffed around the benches. He found a few greasy wrappers and licked the oil off them. There was a dropped muffin that he swallowed in three bites, and pieces of an egg sandwich that tasted as though it had been laying around for a week. But even old and stale and almost rotten, it was still delicious to Benji.

He had just found a half-eaten pulled pork sandwich and was about to head back to his alley to share it with the tiny dog, when he noticed a cat sprinting full tilt toward him. The cat yowled as he ran and turned his head to hiss at his pursuers. He was old and grizzled, with thick, matted black fur that ended in four white paws covered in grime. His yellow eyes glared at the danger behind him.

The cat plunged past Benji and leapt onto a tree. His claws scrabbled at the bark as he climbed up to a bough that hovered at least ten feet in the air.

Benji turned and saw what the cat had been running from. Five stray dogs were loping into the park, their tongues lolling out as they panted in the early morning heat. They streamed past Benji and circled the tree. Their leader was a short-haired dog who had a good fifty pounds on Benji. This dog sat on his haunches and gave a long howl. Five pairs of eyes gazed up at the skinny, spitting cat above them.

Benji thought fast. He dropped the sandwich and gave a short bark. The other dogs turned toward him. Benji picked up the sandwich and then dropped it again. The leader's ears pricked up. With the cat forgotten, he began walking softly toward Benji, with the other four dogs close behind.

Benji gathered up the sandwich between his front teeth and ran. He jumped over bushes and neatly arranged rows of flowers, splashed through a fountain, and emerged dripping but still holding his snack, with the other dogs in hot pursuit. He fled to the other side of the park and darted onto the busy sidewalk, with the dogs running behind him.

He wove through the early morning walkers who were strolling along, and dodged baby strollers and pigeons pecking at crumbs. When he came to the block where his alley was, he circled it three times, until he couldn't see the dogs anymore. Then he jumped into the alley and laid the sandwich at the little dog's feet.

While the little dog munched on her breakfast, Benji headed back toward the park. He found the cat wrapped around the branch, proudly but fearfully gazing at Benji.

Benji spotted an empty stroller next to a park bench near the tree. A mom was teaching her toddler to walk in the grass. Her back was turned to Benji.

While the mother was distracted, Benji pushed the stroller off the walkway and onto the grass below the tree. He looked up at the cat and wagged his tail.

The cat looked doubtful. He dipped a paw down as though he was going to jump, but then drew it back.

"Hey!" The mother had noticed her missing stroller and was coming straight for it.

Benji barked urgently and pawed at the tree.

The cat scrunched up his skinny body and launched into the air. His front feet hit the stroller hood, followed by his hind legs. Another leap, and he was safely down to the ground, just as the mother caught up to the stroller. With hand waves and shouts, she chased Benji and the cat away.

As Benji headed back toward his alley, the cat followed him. When he reached the alley, the cat slunk in behind him.

The tiny dog approached the cat cautiously, her tail wagging. The cat promptly started cleaning the dog's head with his rough, deliberate tongue.

Benji smiled. He liked his growing little pack.

Morning turned into afternoon, and as the summer heat settled down around them, the three friends napped in the alley. The only sounds were flies buzzing lazily around the garbage cans and the sudden snorts the sleeping cat would make.

Suddenly, Benji heard a growl coming from the alley entrance. It was the leader of the dog pack that had chased the cat up the tree—and his four friends. They had found him. They fanned out, blocking the entire alley entrance.

Benji sprang to his feet, looking for a way to defend the old cat and the Chihuahua. But when he looked over to where they had been snoozing a moment ago, they were both gone. It looked like he was going to have to face the pack alone.

The lead dog rushed toward him. Benji sidestepped him and flew down the alley, straight toward the other dogs. As they closed in on him, an enormous, terrifying bark came out of the tin garbage can. It was deep and hollow and full of menace.

The dogs stopped rushing Benji. Their tails sank between their legs.

Another loud, menacing bark exploded out of the can, followed by a horrific growl.

Slowly, the pack backed away. As they retreated, the other garbage can's lid lifted up and fell, rattling on the ground. A paw swooped down and a razor-sharp cat's claw swiped the leader on top of his nose.

Howling, the leader of the pack turned tail and ran out of the alley, with his pack close behind.

Benji went up to the garbage can and stood up on his hind legs to look inside. The tiny dog was at the bottom of the can, grinning at him. She gave a little bark. The sides of the can amplified the sound, making her yip sound like the booming bark of a dog twenty times her size.

That night, as the three animals settled in their alley, Benji fell asleep feeling happy and protected. Even though he hadn't found his family, he didn't feel so alone anymore.

CHAPTER 5

Benji woke to the sound of tiny little yips coming from the Chihuahua. He leapt to his feet and turned straight into the dog pack—which had grown by three. There were now eight strays circling him. The tiny dog and the cat were on top of the garbage cans, hissing and barking, but they were no match for the bigger, tougher pack.

The lead dog circled around Benji. Just as he was about to leap, a van pulled up and screeched to a halt in front of the alley, blocking the entrance. Two humans appeared. One of them carried a pole with a loop that Benji was sure he had seen before. He looked up and recognized the face of the human carrying it. It was the same face of the man who had taken his mother and brothers and sisters and driven off into the night.

The animal catcher swiftly caught the lead dog with his loop. His partner had the same tool and took another member of the pack. As they were loading the dogs into the van, Benji skittered out of the alley, with the tiny dog and the cat darting out behind him.

Just as he was about to escape, Benji came to a sudden halt. Those animal catchers knew where his family was. They had to.

He turned back and peered around the alley. The animal catchers were loading two more dogs into the van. When they had caught all of the members of the dog pack, they hopped into the front of the van and took off.

Benji barked apologetically to his friends and then took off after the van. This time, he was determined not to lose it.

He followed the van through the streets. Luckily for him, the traffic slowed the van down so he was able to keep up with it. Winding through the city, he swerved out of the way of traffic and people, always keeping the gray van in sight.

After what seemed like hours, the van slowed down and turned into a side street. Benji was just about to follow it when he noticed a familiar mop of curly hair across the street. It was Harry. He was in the school playground. He was surrounded by Sam and his gang. Sam had Harry's guitar and was holding it out of his reach. There was no adult in sight.

Benji turned toward the van just as it disappeared from view. He knew he was so close to finding out where his family was. He could leave Harry to the boys and rejoin his mom and his brothers and sisters.

Or he could help the kid who had fed and protected him.

For a moment, he stood, undecided. Then he heard one of the kids laugh. It was a mean, threatening laugh.

In that moment, Benji knew that he couldn't leave the kid alone. It didn't matter that his family could be around the next corner—Harry had been good and generous to him, and he was now in danger.

Benji's family could wait, but Harry couldn't.

Benji made his choice. He turned away from the van and headed across the street.

CHAPTER 6

When Benji arrived, Harry was trying to jump up and reach his guitar. But Sam was just too tall for him.

"You thought you could fool me by giving your guitar to your little friend, didn't you?" Sam sneered. "Well, hotshot musician, you didn't. I found her and I took it and now it's mine!"

"Give that back, Sam!" Harry shouted. His voice was brave, but his face was scared.

"Make me," Sam taunted. The guitar was far out of Harry's reach. "You know, I have half a mind to break this dumb thing."

Harry's face went pale. Benji didn't know what they were saying, but he knew instantly that his friend was in trouble. He looked around and saw Riley at the other end of the playground. She seemed like she was looking for someone.

Benji darted to Riley, barking as hard as he could. When she turned toward him, he wagged his tail and ran toward Harry.

Riley straightened up when she saw what was happening. "There they are," she muttered. She ran toward the cluster of boys.

"Sam! Give that guitar back!" she yelled. Before he could react, she tackled him. She was much smaller, but had the element of surprise. Sam tumbled to the ground. As he did, the guitar fell out of his hands. Benji jumped under it and let it fall softly on his back. It slid off, and Riley caught it before it fell onto the hard playground tar. She leapt to her feet. She took in the situation—four older boys against herself and Harry. "Run, Harry!" she called.

Together, Riley and Harry booked it out of the playground with Benji running next to them. Although they weren't as tough as the guys, they were definitely faster. They took off, running through the city streets, until Sam and the other boys faded into the distance.

Finally, they stopped. Benji looked around. They were in the same park where he had rescued the old cat. Riley put a hand on Harry's shoulder. "Are you all right?"

Harry dropped his head. "Yeah. But look, maybe you should stay out of this. I can take care of myself."

Riley arched her eyebrows. "Are you sure? It didn't seem that way just five minutes ago."

"Yeah, I'm sure," said Harry. "Thanks for trying to help me, but this is boy stuff."

Riley's eyes went wide. "Boy stuff?" she shouted. "It's not boy stuff. It's friend stuff. But if you don't want a girl stopping you from getting beaten up, fine."

Harry drew back. "I didn't mean—"

"Yes, you did mean that," Riley shot back. She thrust the guitar toward Harry. "Here. Take it. And if Sam and his hooligans bother you again, don't count on me to save you." She let go of the guitar and stalked off.

"Wait," Harry called.

Riley kept going. She didn't look back.

Harry sank onto one of the park benches and dropped the guitar next to him. He put his head in his hands. "I can't do anything right," he groaned.

Benji nudged his knee. Harry looked up and smiled. "Hey, pup." He patted an empty spot on the bench, and Benji jumped up, laying his head against Harry's side.

Harry sighed. "Why can't life be simpler?" he said. He stroked Benji's matted fur. "All I want to do is play guitar. But every time I try to play in school, Sam and his gang show up and start picking on me. I can't even get three chords out before they find me. It's as if they have a supernatural sense of when

I'm trying to play with an audience." With his free hand, Harry touched the guitar strings. "There's a talent show coming up that I really want to perform in, but every time I try to play, I think that Sam's going to get me. It has gotten to the point where my hands start to shake just thinking about it." He held up his hand. "See?"

Benji nudged his head into Harry's trembling hand. He kept it there until he could feel the boy's fingers gently turn steady.

Harry smiled down at Benji. "You're a pretty special dog, you know that? Somehow, when I'm around you, I don't feel so scared."

A curious squirrel jumped onto the park bench and made a flying leap toward the guitar. Benji stood up and barked. The squirrel changed direction in midair and landed next to the guitar instead of on it. In a flash, it scurried off the bench. Benji gave a short, satisfied woof.

Harry laughed. "So, you're my guitar guardian, is that it?"

Benji raised his eyes and nodded.

"All right. If you protect me, I'll play for you." Harry picked up the guitar. Benji leapt down from the bench. Strutting back and forth, he began to walk in front of Harry like a guard on duty.

A chord sang out of the guitar. Then a second, and a third . . . and a fourth. Sam did not appear.

Neither did his bullying friends. As the morning turned into afternoon, and then early evening, and the sun sank behind the city buildings, a boy sat in his own little world, picking out a tune on his guitar while a golden-haired stray kept watch.

CHAPTER 7

The next day, Benji was waiting for Harry—and he had brought some company. He had gone hunting for food with his alley friends, and had just found a half-eaten foot-long hot dog to share with them when he remembered that Harry usually got out of school around that time. Trotting over to the playground, he dropped his lunch and greeted Harry with a woof. Harry was carrying a backpack on his shoulders and holding his guitar.

"Who are your friends?" Harry asked when he saw the tiny dog and the gnarled cat gobbling down the hot dog. He bent down and patted the cat, then took one of his white paws in his hand. "You look like a Mittens."

Benji wagged his tail. Mittens sounded like a perfect name for the old cat.

When Harry reached for the Chihuahua, though, the little dog swallowed the last bite of the hot dog and ducked away. "Where are you going, Tiny?" Harry asked.

Tiny scurried behind a tree.

"Shy little girl, aren't you?" said Harry. "Well, that's all right. I'm a little shy, too." He held up his guitar and beckoned to Benji. "Want to come help me practice?" With his other hand, he dug into his backpack and pulled out a tuna fish sandwich. "I've got a snack!"

Benji wagged his tail. He and the other animals followed Harry, past the playground and into the park, where he tossed them the sandwich to munch on. Afterward, Tiny hid underneath a bench out of reach from strangers while Benji and Mittens sat next to Harry as he strummed his guitar, working out the right tune for the talent show. The melody became stronger, and Benji and Mittens started nodding their heads to the beat.

Harry laughed when he saw them. "Thanks for the encouragement, guys. I've almost worked it all out, but it would sound even better on two guitars. I wish I had one more person playing a few chords."

As the afternoon turned into evening, Harry got up to go home. He studied Benji thoughtfully. "You know, you've helped me a lot these past couple of days. Before you came along, I couldn't have ever dreamed that I'd feel safe enough to practice in the open." He bent down to pat Benji on the head.

"Harry! What are you doing with those animals?" a voice called out.

Benji turned to see an older man hurrying toward them. He had the same brown curly hair and green eyes as Harry. "Stay away from those mutts!" he shouted.

Harry shot to his feet. He stepped in front of Benji, Mittens, and Tiny. "But, Dad, they've been helping me!"

"Helping you by giving you rabies and fleas and ticks and who knows what else?" Harry's father took out a bottle of hand sanitizer and tossed it to his son. "Use that immediately!" he demanded.

Harry shook his head. "Dad, just because you're scared of germs doesn't mean that—"

"I don't want to hear excuses," said Harry's dad. "Now, hurry!"

Harry sighed. He popped open the sanitizer cap and squeezed out of dollop of clear liquid. He slathered it over his hands and then closed the bottle. "There. Happy?"

"I'd be happier if you didn't touch strays," said his dad.

"They're fine, Dad!" protested Harry.

His dad shook his head. "No, they're not." He shuddered. "Who knows what kind of bugs they're carrying?"

Harry sighed. "Okay, look. I'm practicing for the school talent show tomorrow night, and these animals help me feel less nervous. Can we come to some sort of deal?" He held up the sanitizer. "How about I can have them stay with me in the park, but they don't go home with me, and I put this goop on my hands when I'm finished practicing."

His dad paused for a long moment. "The talent show is tomorrow?"

"Yes," said Harry.

"And you won't need them after the show?"

Harry hesitated. "Well, not to help me practice."

"And you'll promise me you'll clean your hands the instant you're done?"

Harry nodded. "I promise."

His dad shrugged. "All right. But if I catch any one of those animals at home, deal's over. No more park, and no more guitar playing." He dug into his pocket. "Keep the one you have—I've got extra," he said, holding up a second bottle of sanitizer. He stuck it back in his pocket and walked away.

Harry sank onto the park bench. "That was close. For a second I thought he'd say no to everything." He scratched underneath Benji's and Mittens' chins. "I'd adopt you all in a heartbeat if my dad would let me, but he's the boss at home." He tucked his guitar under his arm. "Well, that's enough practice for one day. I'll see you guys tom—"

Before Harry finished speaking, Benji had taken off.

Benji had spotted a familiar four-legged creature at the far side of the park. She was long-haired and scruffy, and had a pretty blue collar wrapped around her neck. She was being walked by a plump older lady with fluffy gray hair and a shawl around her shoulders.

Everything in Benji's world had disappeared into one mission—catching up to the dog and the lady, who were leaving the park. He was certain that he recognized the soft brown eyes and long, beautiful fur. It had to be his mother. It just had to be. He ran, barking with all of his might, trying to get her attention—or at the very least, slow her down.

His long nails clacked against the park's well-worn path. Pigeons and squirrels darted out of his way. With every leap, he got a little closer to his mother, until he jumped in front of her, his tail wagging hard and his mouth open in a joyous welcome bark.

The bark died in his throat. The dog he had caught up with was a stranger. She looked at him curiously, but without any recognition whatsoever.

"Shoo!" her owner said, batting Benji away.

Benji's tail drooped. His eyes fell and his head sagged. He slumped under a bench and put his paws over his face. For a few precious moments, he thought that his quest to find his family was over. Now all he had was disappointment.

After a while, he felt someone pick him up and settle onto the bench. It was Harry. "Now I understand," he said as Tiny and Mittens joined them. "You weren't looking for a home, buddy, were you? You were looking for your family." He held Benji in his arms until the long, slow afternoon shadows deepened into evening. Then, with a final pat, Harry got up and left for his home, leaving Benji gathered around the park bench with Mittens and Tiny.

CHAPTER 8

The next afternoon, Benji, Tiny, and Mittens met Harry at the school playground. "No more practicing in the park today," Harry told Benji. "Tonight is the talent show!" He waved at the three animals to follow him. "Come with me. I want to thank you for helping me get over my stage fright."

Harry led the animals through the streets and stopped at a familiar bakery. Benji pricked up his ears with surprise. The bakery was the same one that was right across from the alley where the animals had been staying.

"Wait here," Harry told them. He ducked inside and then came out with three humungous pieces of ham-and-cheese pie. He set them down in front of the animals. "Eat up, guys!"

As they were gulping down their meal, Benji

heard a sound coming from across the street. His eyebrows furrowed. Something—or someone—was in their alley. He swallowed a last bit of pie and then swiftly trotted over to investigate.

He poked his head into the alley. He heard muffled sobs coming from behind the last garbage can.

Slowly, Benji walked into the alley and peered around the can.

Sam was sitting on the pavement, hugging his knees to his chest. His head was down and his shoulders were shaking.

Benji gently laid his paw on Sam's shoe. Sam looked up. He sniffed. "Hey, mutt," he said gruffly. "What are you doing here?"

Benji crept a little closer. He licked away the tears that were streaked across Sam's face.

Despite himself, Sam laughed. He reached out and scratched behind Benji's ears. "Lucky dog. You don't have to be human. You don't have to deal with being bullied every time you want to do something you love."

He closed his eyes and leaned his head against the brick wall. "All I ever wanted to do was play music. But when you've got an older brother who mocks you every time you mention the 'm' word, you start to accept the fact that your dreams will be squashed even before they've begun."

Sam opened his eyes and took a long look at

Benji. "You know, I'm going to tell you a secret. You won't tell anyone, I guess. There's a kid I keep picking on in school. He's pretty good with the guitar. In fact, he's really good. The truth is, I'm just jealous that he's allowed to practice when I can't."

"Is that why you've been picking on me all this time?" Harry stood in the alleyway, holding the guitar down at his feet.

Sam jumped up. "If you tell anyone I've been crying . . ."

Harry shook his head. "I won't. Hey, I'm sorry about your brother. I didn't know you liked music." He held out the guitar. "If you want, I can teach you how to play."

Sam shook his head. "Wouldn't work. My brother would know the second I was practicing with you in school."

"It doesn't have to be in school," said Harry. "I could teach you in the afternoons, at my place."

"You would do that for me?" asked Sam.

Harry nodded. "Sure. Music is something that everyone should have the chance to try." He stuck out his hand. "How about every day after school you come to my place for an hour. We'll borrow a guitar from the school. I can teach you some chords and we can jam. Deal?"

Benji looked at the two boys. For a moment, they were utterly still. Harry's hand was still waiting to shake on it. Benji woofed and pawed at Sam's leg. Then he shook his paw with Harry.

Sam laughed. When Benji dropped his paw, he took Harry's hand in his. "Deal."

"C'mon. We've got a talent show to get to." Harry and Sam headed back to the school, with Benji trotting behind them.

CHAPTER 9

"How are we going to get the dog inside the school?" Sam asked. He and Harry were in front of the auditorium, watching as people filed in and out of the doors.

Harry's face fell. "I'm not sure." He turned to Benji. "Sorry, buddy, but you might have to miss the show." He pointed to the doors. "There are too many people going to see the performances. I don't think we can sneak you inside."

Benji didn't understand Harry's words, but he could see from the way his shoulders were sagging that something was wrong. He saw the people going inside, and Harry pointing to them. He realized that he couldn't go in with all those people watching.

He trotted around the corner of the school. His eyes lit on a small window that was open on the ground level. He gave a bark to let Harry know where he was and then squeezed through the window. Jumping down from the painted sill, he found himself in a large room filled with instruments.

"Nice work!" Harry told Benji through the window. "You stay put. We'll go through the doors and meet you in a second."

A few moments later, Harry and Sam appeared in the music room. Benji had gone up to one of the guitars on a stand at the front of the room. He woofed at Harry and Sam.

"What are you trying to tell us, buddy?" Harry asked.

Benji pawed at the side of the guitar. Then he went over and pawed at Sam's pant leg.

Harry smiled. "I think what he's trying to say is that you should join me in my act for the talent show."

Sam shook his head. "I can't. I don't know how to play."

Harry picked up the guitar and handed it to Sam. Then he slung his own guitar around his neck and put his fingers to the strings. "Follow my lead," he instructed Sam.

Together, the two boys practiced a chord progression. "You're pretty good!" Harry said.

Sam smiled. "Thanks, man."

"When we get up there, I'll start playing. Whenever I nod to you, play these three chords," Harry said.

"Got it," Sam replied.

"Let's get to the show!" said Harry.

The boys stuck their heads out of the music room. The coast was clear. Running through the hallways, Harry, Sam, and Benji came to the backstage entrance to the auditorium. The show had already started, and no one was at the door.

"C'mon," whispered Harry. He opened the door and let Benji inside. He hid behind a rack of costumes in the wings.

Harry was the last act in the show. Benji watched as he walked on stage and faced the audience. "I'd like to play an original song for you," he said. "But I'm going to need a little help from my friend Sam." He turned toward the wings and motioned for Sam to come on stage.

In the wings, Sam stood frozen. He was clutching the guitar, unable to move his feet. When Harry waved for him to come out, he shook his head. His face had gone white.

Benji sprang into action. He snuck up behind Sam and licked the back of his knees.

Surprised, Sam stumbled forward—right onto the stage. As the audience clapped, he turned toward

Benji. His eyes were big and dark and full of fear. His hands were trembling.

Benji woofed and stuck his tongue out. He gave Sam the biggest, goofiest smile he could.

Sam laughed. His hands relaxed and stopped shaking. He joined Harry at the center of the stage. "Let's do this," he said. Together they faced the audience.

Benji heard the first notes of the song Harry had practiced in the park. As the music spilled through the auditorium, he looked out. He could see people starting to smile.

Harry nodded to Sam. A moment later, the sound of two guitars filled the room. It was magnificent.

As Harry and Sam played, people in the audience began to get up and move to the beat of the music. Soon the whole place was filled with people dancing and cheering and yelling over the waves of music coming from the stage.

With a final drawn-out chord, Harry and Sam ended their piece. They stood basking in the spotlight, sweat sliding down their foreheads, grinning at each other.

Backstage, Benji howled happily. He watched as Harry and Sam took a bow and then rejoined him behind the curtains.

A few moments later, the principal came to the

microphone. “The winner . . . or rather winners . . . of tonight’s talent show are Harry and Sam!”

As students and their parents headed home for the night, Benji, Harry, and Sam stood next to the exit doors. Warm yellow lamplight surrounded them and a soft wind blew through their hair.

Sam shuffled his feet. “Hey, thanks for including me in your act tonight.”

Harry nodded. “It was great, man.”

Sam bent down and ruffled Benji’s fur. “And thanks for giving me that nudge forward. Otherwise I would have been frozen backstage forever.”

“Hey, Sam!” Benji turned and saw an older boy heading their way. He had muscles as big as hubcaps and looked like he could bench-press a car.

“Uh, hey, Bobby,” Sam said. Nervously, he shoved the guitar that he had been holding at Harry. “He’s the brother I told you about,” he hissed.

Bobby approached them. He lifted a big meaty hand.

Sam winced.

Bobby brought his hand down on his brother’s shoulder and shook him excitedly. “Dude, you were awesome! Where’d you learn to play like that?”

Sam stopped looking like he was about to faint. “Harry taught me,” he said weakly.

Bobby turned to Harry. "Hey, man. I've teased my kid brother a lot about loving music. Thought it was pretty stupid stuff. But tonight, you guys rocked out hard. It was like, seriously, the best song I've heard . . . ever!" He folded his arms. "So. Do you think you could teach me?"

Harry swallowed. "Teach you?"

"Yeah! How to play like you!" said Bobby.

Harry smiled. "Sure. But under one condition. Sam gets to learn, too."

Bobby stuck his hand out. "Deal."

As they shook on it, Riley came up to them. "Nice job, Harry," she said.

Harry blushed. "Thanks, Riley."

"You weren't half bad, either," Riley told Sam. She smiled. "Hey, listen. If you ever want to get together sometime and play some music, maybe we could start a band. You know, the three of us."

"Can it be four?" asked Bobby.

Riley eyed him. "Depends, tough guy. You practice real hard, and then you come to me in a month and I'll decide."

For a moment, Bobby's face went red and it looked like he was going to explode. Then he nodded. "You got it," he said.

"Harry! I'm so proud of you!" Harry's dad came striding down the hallway. He gave Harry a big hug. "You're a natural at the guitar."

"Actually, it wasn't just talent." Harry bent down and patted Benji on the head. "If it wasn't for this guy, I wouldn't have had the courage to get up there. He's the one who made me feel safe while I practiced in the park. I pretended he was the audience, and after a while I didn't feel so scared of playing my music. And," he continued, giving Benji an extra-deep scratch, "I didn't catch any germs or fleas or anything for the whole week."

"Did you use the hand sanitizer?" his dad asked.

"I did," said Harry.

"Well, here goes nothing," said his dad. He knelt down and gingerly laid his hand on Benji's head. Benji woofed and rolled over, waving his paws in the air. Laughing, Harry's dad began scratching Benji's tummy. As he was scratching, Benji saw two familiar friends trotting toward him. Mittens and Tiny had followed him, on their own, all the way to the school. Mittens was in the lead, with Tiny following skittishly behind. When Tiny saw the cluster of humans gathered around Benji, she yelped and jumped behind a lamppost.

"Sox!" cried Bobby when he saw Mittens. He went straight to the cat. Ignoring his yowls, he scooped him up and cradled him in his arms. "Where have you been?"

"You know him?" Harry asked in disbelief.

Bobby nodded. "He's mine. Crazy old furball

jumped out of an open window a few weeks ago and I've been looking for him ever since." He brought his head down and touched his nose to the cat's. "Let's go home and get you some dinner," he told the purring Sox.

Harry's dad nodded toward Tiny's trembling ears, which were the only things he could see. "And who's this?"

Harry ducked his head. "Oh, that's Tiny. I've never seen her up close. She's too scared of people to let anyone get near her."

"I have an idea." His dad reached into his pocket and pulled out a Slim Jim. He peeled down the plastic wrapper and pulled off a chunk of the jerky. He went to the lamppost and crouched down. He gently tossed the chunk to Tiny. It landed in front of her feet.

Tiny bent down and sniffed the jerky. Her eyes lit up and a little pink tongue stuck out. With one gulp, she downed the treat.

Harry's dad broke off another piece and tossed it, only a little closer to himself. Bit by bit, he coaxed Tiny out from her hiding spot. Finally, he took the remaining half of the Slim Jim and laid it in front of his feet. Tiny stood still for a moment. Then she trotted forward and began to gnaw on the stick.

Harry's dad reached down and he patted her back softly. Tiny bolted upright. But as Harry's dad kept patting her, her tiny muscles began to relax. Harry's dad held out his hand. Tiny sniffed it and then began to lick his fingers. When she was done, he gathered her into his arms. "Guess we're both learning how to overcome our fears tonight," he said.

CHAPTER 10

As the last of the showgoers left the auditorium, Harry and his father started for home.

Benji and Tiny followed. Benji had never seen Tiny connect to another human the way she had with Harry's father. He knew that if she had any chance of getting off the streets, going home with Harry and his dad was her best shot.

As they passed the alley where they had lived, Tiny turned into it and began to head toward her spot behind the garbage can. Benji leapt in front of her and barked. He couldn't let her stay—not when she could be going home with a family that would love her and keep her safe.

Tiny barked back and tried to scurry around Benji. Benji lowered his head and scooped her up like a kitten. Paying no mind to her surprised yelps, he trotted out of the alley and fell in line behind Harry and his dad. When they paused at a crosswalk, Benji put her down and nudged her toward Harry's dad.

For a moment, Tiny looked longingly back toward the alley. Then she turned her head and ran up next to Harry's dad's feet. He looked down. "You two are following us home, huh?" he said. His voice was gruff, but there was a smile buried in there.

Benji and Tiny followed Harry and his dad through the city until they turned onto the corner where the two humans lived. As Harry and his dad began climbing the stoop stairs, Benji gave Tiny a final nudge to follow them.

Harry's dad fished a ring of keys out of his pocket. He put one in the slot and opened the front door wide. "Coming in?" he asked Tiny.

Tiny looked frantically at Benji. Benji woofed encouragingly. She woofed back and followed Harry's dad inside.

Harry sat down with Benji on the stoop. "Do you want to stay with us, too?" he asked. He motioned up the steps to the entrance of his place. "We could give you a real nice home."

Benji stood looking at the open door. He knew he could follow Tiny in and be warm and safe and loved. But there was still a part of him that wanted—needed—his freedom. A home would be wonderful, but his family was still out there. He wanted to find them. And, as hard as the alley had been, he had been able to do whatever he wanted, whenever he wanted. He had a feeling that he wasn't done with exploring and adventuring. The road he had started on, which had seemed so long and scary, was beckoning him now. It wanted him to keep on moving and keep on traveling until he was sure that he was ready to settle down.

Benji reached up and licked Harry's face. Then he made his way down the steps. He looked back one final time and woofed.

Harry nodded. "I get it. When you chased that dog in the park, I should have figured you'd still want to be looking for your family. It's all right." He brought the guitar onto his knees and began strumming. "I'll miss you, but I know you've got to go," he sang.

Benji smiled. He had learned a lot from his days in the city. He had found a place to sleep and defended it from bullies. He had formed a pack and kept them safe. He had befriended a human and helped him overcome his fears. And most important, he had learned how brave he could be. He felt proud of the dog he was becoming.

As he trotted down the street into the great unknown, with his tail wagging high, Harry's voice followed him. It was a good voice. A voice that he would remember always.